My Freedom Trip

by Frances Park and Ginger Park
Illustrated by Debra Reid Jenkins

Boyds Mills Press

For our mother and her mother
—F.P. and G.P.

To the courageous people of Korea and other nations who have risked their lives
to obtain not only their own freedom but also the freedom of others...
they are the true heroes
—D.R.J.

Korean words used in this story:
Apa: Father, Papa
Oma: Mother, Mama
yut: a Korean board game played with sticks

Korean characters in the order they appear in this book:

평화 Peace	사랑 Love	희망 Hope
속삼임들 Whispers	여행 Journey	용기 Bravery
약속 Promise	듣기 Listen	자유 Freedom
기다림 Waiting	위험 Danger	전쟁 War
두려움 Fear	그리움 Longing	

Text copyright © 1998 by Frances Park and Ginger Park
Illustrations copyright © 1998 by Debra Reid Jenkins
All rights reserved

Published by Caroline House
Boyds Mills Press, Inc.
A Highlights Company
815 Church Street
Honesdale, Pennsylvania 18431

Printed in Mexico

Publisher Cataloging-in-Publication Data
Park, Frances
My freedom trip / by Frances Park and Ginger Park ; illustrated
by Debra R. Jenkins.—1st ed.
[32]p. : col. ill. ; cm.
Summary: Based on the life of the authors' mother, this is the story of
her escape from North Korea.
ISBN 1-56397-468-1
1. Korea (North)—Biography—Juvenile literature.
[1. Korea (North)—Biography.] I. Park, Ginger. II. Jenkins, Debra R., ill. III. Title.
951.93 / 92-dc21   1998   AC   CIP
Library of Congress Catalog Card Number 97-77911

First edition, 1998
Book design by Amy Drinker, Aster Designs
The text of this book is set in 15-point Tiepolo.
The illustrations are done in oils on canvas.
10 9 8 7 6 5 4 3 2 1

*Many years ago, when I was a little schoolgirl
in Korea, soldiers invaded my country. The soldiers
drew a big line that divided Korea into two
countries, North Korea and South Korea. In North
Korea we could no longer speak our minds, or
come and go as we pleased. We lost our freedom.
Many of us secretly escaped to South Korea,
the freedom land. This is my story....*

평화

A peaceful sun shone upon my village in North Korea, over rice paddies and pagoda roofs, on pink petals in ponds and quartz stones on the ground.

I walked home from school, down a path where flowering bushes lined the road and a soft breeze carried butterflies.

It was a beautiful day. The sky seemed endless, and my eyes were soaring! From here, the world looked as free as the doves swiftly dipping into treetops.

But one by one my classmates had been missing from school. First Eumi, then Eunook, then Miyook. My best friends! They had left their homes in the middle of the night to cross the border to the freedom land.

Now I walked home alone.

속삭임들

Then one night my father came to my room and gently woke me. It was so dark that I could not see his face. He spoke softly.

"Tonight I must go on a trip. A man named Mr. Han will guide me to South Korea. He knows of a secret passage where I will cross the border at the shallow end of a river."

"*Apa*," I wailed, "do not go!"

My father stroked my hair. His fingers were trembling. "Soon, very soon, Mr. Han will return for you, Soo. And he will take you on your freedom trip. Then it will be your mother's turn."

"But why can't we go together?" I pleaded.

"Only one of us can go at a time," he tried to explain. "Less people means less danger of being captured by soldiers."

What was *danger*? It sounded as deep and dark and cold as a river.

My father kissed my cheek, then left my side. He stood in the doorway for a long time.

"I will be waiting for you on the other side of the river," he promised.

기다림

My mother and I awaited word of my father. Every morning we sipped barley tea, wondering where he was. Every evening we played *yut*, still wondering.

One evening full of moon and warm winds, we heard a *tap, tap, tap*.

My mother dropped her *yut* sticks and rushed to open the door.

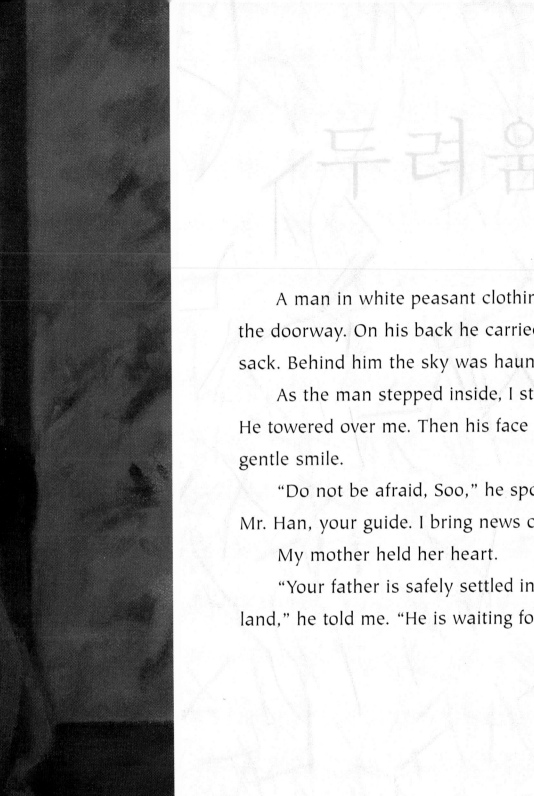

A man in white peasant clothing stood in the doorway. On his back he carried a big heavy sack. Behind him the sky was haunting.

As the man stepped inside, I stepped back. He towered over me. Then his face broke into a gentle smile.

"Do not be afraid, Soo," he spoke. "I am Mr. Han, your guide. I bring news of your father."

My mother held her heart.

"Your father is safely settled in the freedom land," he told me. "He is waiting for you."

사랑

My mother quietly rejoiced, then began packing my knapsack with jelly candy, fruit, and clothing.

"Tonight you go on your freedom trip, Soo," she carefully announced. "Now quickly, you must change your clothes."

"*Oma,*" I begged, "come with me!"

She cupped my face and whispered, "Do not worry." Her breath was as warm and soothing as tea. "Mr. Han will return for me, and we will be reunited."

My mother hugged me. I could feel her heart beating against mine like a dying dove.

"Be brave, Soo!" she cried.

여행

My freedom trip began by train.

Mr. Han took my hand. Silently, we boarded.
The train was crowded with passengers bumping
into one another. No one spoke or let their
eyes meet.

I looked out the window. Farms and villages
seemed to speed by me. Already I missed my
mother's touch. Already our parting seemed like
a lifetime ago!

The train came to a stop at the foot of a tall, rocky mountain. Mr. Han secretly nodded. Then we slipped away from the train and into the night.

Up the mountain we walked, with the cries of wild animals in our ears and the moon in our eyes. The woods were all around us.

Every few moments, Mr. Han would stop and listen for footsteps. I would listen, too.

We were as still as rocks.

Then he would wink at me and we would continue up the mountain.

위험

All at once footsteps were upon us!

Mr. Han and I crouched in bushes, not breathing. We watched the long shadows of soldiers creep along a row of rocks.

Were we in danger?

When the shadows disappeared and the footsteps grew distant, Mr. Han whispered, "The soldiers can spot our shadows on the ground because the moon is bright tonight." Sorrowfully, he squeezed my hand. "We must hide here, Soo, until the moon has fallen from the sky."

그리움

Mr. Han opened his sack. Then he put a blanket around me and began peeling fruit in the moonlight.

How I longed for my father! How I wished he could come and carry me across the river to the freedom land. How I longed for my mother! How I wished I was back home playing *yut* with her.

In a gust of wind, her last words came to me—*Be brave, Soo*!

In time the moon vanished behind the mountain.

All was dark over Korea. Mr. Han took my hand. We were like owls, looking everywhere.

We walked until daylight touched the mountainside with grass and wildflowers and four-leafed clovers, until the sound of rushing water reached my ears.

"I can hear the river," I whispered.

Mr. Han nodded knowingly. "You are close to freedom, Soo."

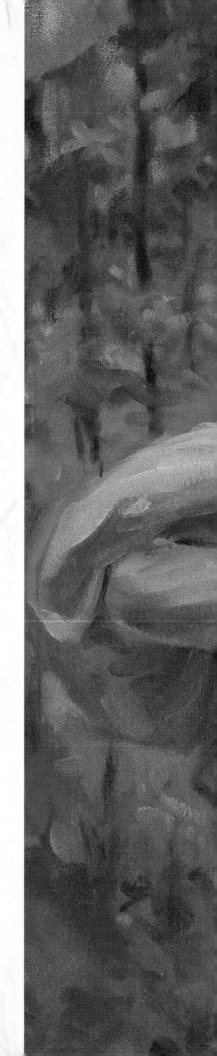

용기

Suddenly, leaves rustled.

We stopped and listened for footsteps. Mr. Han's hand trembled in mine.

Were we in danger?

A soldier leaped into our path! His eyes darkened as he raised his weapon.

"Halt!" he demanded. "Turn around and go back to your village!"

Mr. Han pleaded with him. "I will go back. But please let the child go. Her father is waiting for her across the river."

"No one is allowed to cross the river!" the soldier shouted.

"I beg you, let the child go," Mr. Han continued to plead. "She has come a long way without sleep."

The soldier's attention turned to me. I did not move. I did not speak. The mountain was so quiet I could hear a breeze pass through the trees. It carried my mother's message—
Be brave, Soo!

After a long, silent spell, the soldier lowered his weapon. He looked away from me. I heard him whisper, "Go quickly, child."

Mr. Han guided me toward a dark, mossy opening in the woods. "I must go back, but you are free, Soo. Go! Go!"

I ran without thinking. I was so frightened I forgot where I was going.

Then I saw the river. The water was so blue, my eyes were swimming in every direction! And there was my father, waving wildly from the other side. The freedom land!

"Soo! Soo!" he cried out.

"*Apa!*" I cried back.

I rushed into the river, embracing the sun and the sky.

I was free!

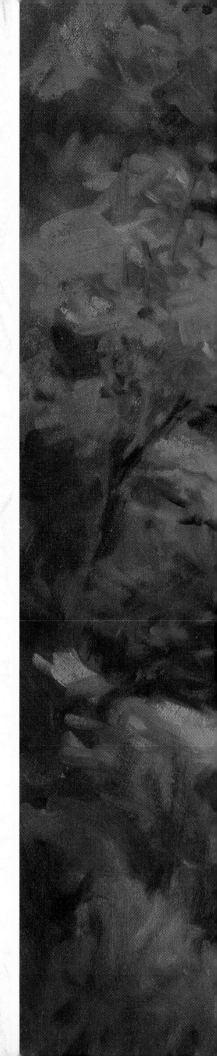

전쟁

Shortly after my freedom trip, soldiers were posted all along the border, and my mother was forced to stay in North Korea.

Soon the Korean War broke out. The war was bigger than any mountain and more haunting than any sky. When the fighting ended, my country was still divided.

I never saw my mother again. How could we have known that the river I crossed would separate us forever?

Many years have passed. I am no longer a little schoolgirl.
But I still think about Mr. Han, my gentle guide,
and about the soldier who set me free.
Mostly, I think about my mother.
When the evening is full of moon and warm winds,
I can still hear her cry—Be brave, Soo!
Brave for the rest of my life.

YAY FOR CLAY!

ART ROOM

SNAKE'S BIG MISTAKE

Sarah Kurpiel

GREENWILLOW BOOKS

An Imprint of HarperCollinsPublishers

The illustrations were created digitally.
The text type is Serifa Standard.

Library of Congress Cataloging-in-Publication Data

Names: Kurpiel, Sarah, author, illustrator.
Title: Snake's big mistake / written and illustrated by Sarah Kurpiel.
Description: First edition. | New York : Greenwillow Books, an Imprint
  of HarperCollins Publishers, [2023] | Audience: Ages 4–8. | Audience:
  Grades K–1. | Summary: Snake loves art class—until his clay pot breaks
  and he makes a terrible decision.
Identifiers: LCCN 2022036361 | ISBN 9780063093218 (hardcover)
Subjects: CYAC: Snakes—Fiction. | Animals—Fiction. | Pottery—Fiction. |
  Friendship—Fiction. | LCGFT: Animal fiction. | Picture books.
Classification: LCC PZ7.1.K87 Sn 2023 | DDC [E]—dc23
LC record available at https://lccn.loc.gov/2022036361
23 24 25 26 27 RTLO 10 9 8 7 6 5 4 3 2 1
First Edition

Greenwillow Books

For my elementary school
art teacher

Snake set out to sculpt the best, most spectacular, positively greatest clay pot in art class.

Week 1: Snake rolled and coiled.

Week 2: He brushed on glaze.

Then it was time to wait. "Next week," said Mr. Owl, "your clay creations will be back from the kiln—shiny, colorful, and ready to take home!"

Snake couldn't wait. Maybe a museum would want to display his masterpiece.

But when he saw his finished pot
alongside all the others . . .

Snake wished he had never seen it at all.
"I've made the *worst* clay pot in art class!"

Snake slid across the room
to sneak the clay pot out of sight.
But up close, he saw something
wasn't right.

Mr. Owl had mixed up "Snake"
and "Turtle."

"Well," whispered Snake, "it
wasn't *my* mistake."

SNAKE

TURTLE

Snake looked to the left.

He looked to the right.

Could he do it?

He was doing it.

Snake did it. He took Turtle's clay pot.
"Your pot is amazing!" said Elephant.
"The best!" said Tiger.

Turtle didn't say anything at all.

"You have a talent for pottery," said Mr. Owl.
Turtle didn't take her usual seat beside Snake.

"We're so proud," said Snake's mom, as she placed
the pot at the center of the table for everyone to see.

But the only thing Snake could think about was Turtle.

That night, Snake couldn't sleep.

Maybe a snack would help, Snake thought. He slithered to the kitchen.

There it was again—Turtle's clay pot,
sitting on the table, staring at him.
Would it be there *forever*?

Snake looked
to the left.

He looked
to the right.

Could he
do it?

He was
doing it.

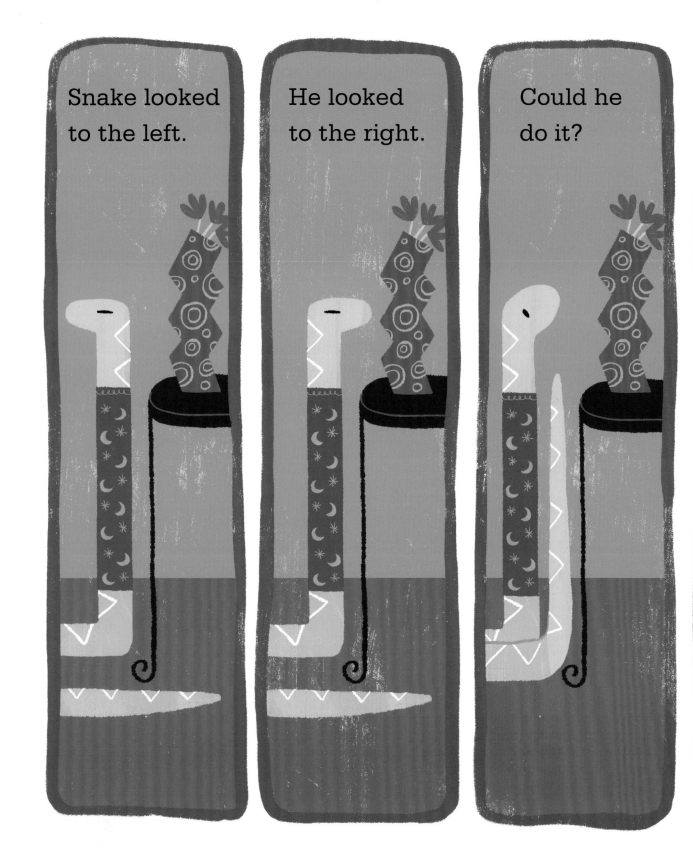

Snake immediately wished he could undo it. Snake wished he could undo

Glue. He needed glue. Quick!
Piece by piece, Snake pasted
Turtle's clay pot back together.
He held it tight until it dried—
and then a little while longer,
just to be sure.

"It looks pretty good," Snake said to himself
as he curled back up in bed. "Tomorrow,
I will make things right."

But the next day, it all went wrong.

"Thanks for apologizing," said Turtle. "But it doesn't change what you did. I thought we were friends. I guess I was wrong."

Snake twisted inside and out.
Some things could not be put back
together with glue.

How could Snake repair
a broken friendship?

By art class, he knew what he had to do.

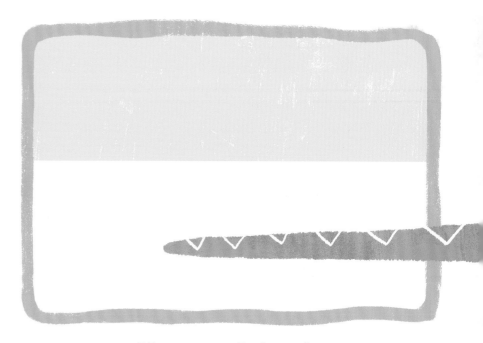

But could he do it?

He was doing it.

Snake did it. He told Mr. Owl the whole story. ". . . and that's why *Turtle* is the one with a talent for pottery, not me. She deserves a chance to redo her project."

Mr. Owl looked at Turtle, then back at Snake.
"Telling me took courage," he said. "I think
you *both* deserve a second chance.
Everything takes practice—even friendship."

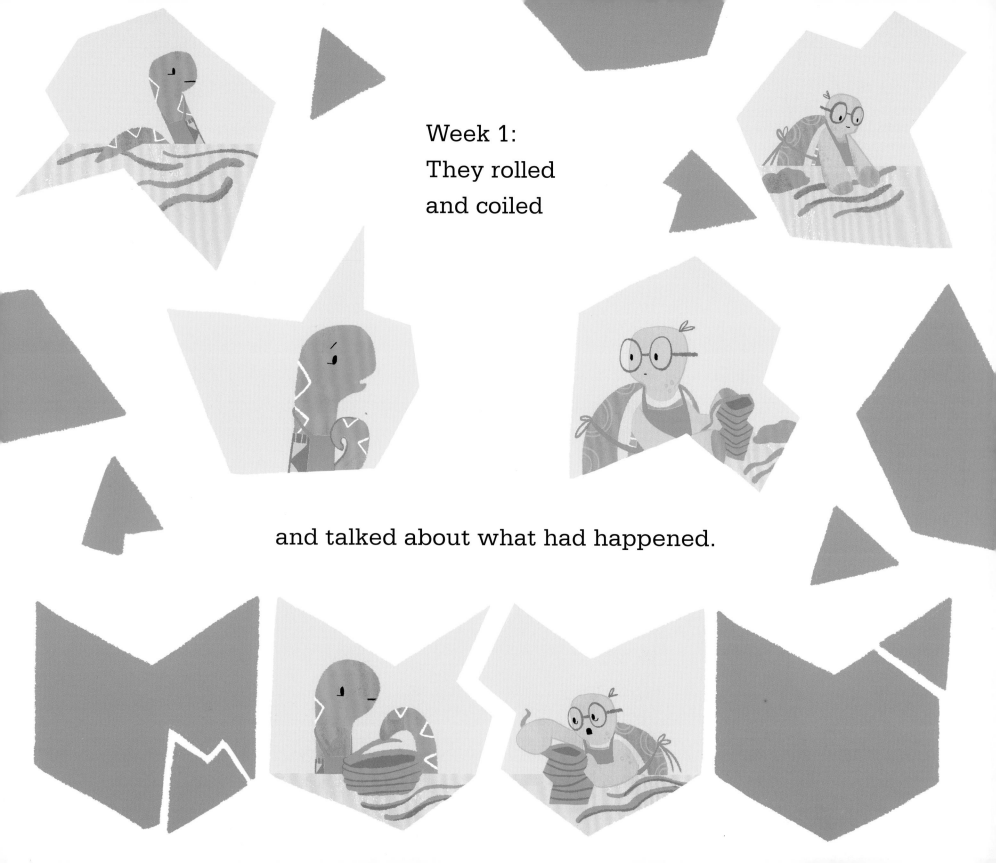

Week 1:
They rolled
and coiled

and talked about what had happened.

Week 2: They brushed on glaze and found they could laugh again.

Then it was time to wait. Together.

This time, when their clay creations came back from the kiln—shiny, colorful, and ready to take home—

Snake made sure everyone knew Turtle had made the best, most spectacular, positively greatest clay pot in art class.

Because it was true. There was no mistaking it. And because that's what good friends do.